Bear cave
for sale
P.O. Box 9214071

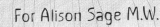

Bear Sports Day
SUNDAY 10AM

BEAR
BOOGIE
Saturday
7PM

For Alison Sage M.W.

Sandy Creek
NEW YORK

An Imprint of Sterling Publishing
387 Park Avenue South
New York, NY 10016

BEAR
FESTIVAL
Friday
1PM

HELP
NEEDED!
Bear Wood
Gardening Day

BEAR WOOD
PICNIC
Sunday 12PM

WANTED
HONEYPOTS
P.O. BOX 93416180

BEAR WOOD

Bears, Bears, Bears!

Martin Waddell and Lee Wildish

Sandy Creek
NEW YORK

Ruby liked bears so she put up a sign.

BEARS WANTED FOR PLAYING with RUBY xx

BEAR WOOD →

Along came a bear.
"I'm a bear from Bear Wood,"
said the bear. "Will I do?"

"You're just what I wanted," said Ruby.
Ruby and the bear played games:

bear hug...

"More bears mean more fun!" cried Ruby. So Ruby's bear sent out to Bear Wood for more bears.

Two little bears came from Bear Wood and they played with Ruby.

"More! More!" cried Ruby. So Ruby's bear sent out to Bear Wood again and a bunch of party-loving, ring-a-ding bears turned up.

One cool bear played the piano and sang, and some of them danced on the patio.

They all wanted to dance with Ruby, and they whirled and twirled until she was tuckered out.

But she still cried,

"More! More! More!"
And more and more bears came from Bear Wood.

Some of them took Ruby swimming down at the creek.

The moon rose over Bear Wood
as Ruby came sleepily home.

Back at her house, the bear party was still going on. There were bears in the cupboards and bears on the stairs. Bears looking at pictures and climbing on chairs. There were bears everywhere!

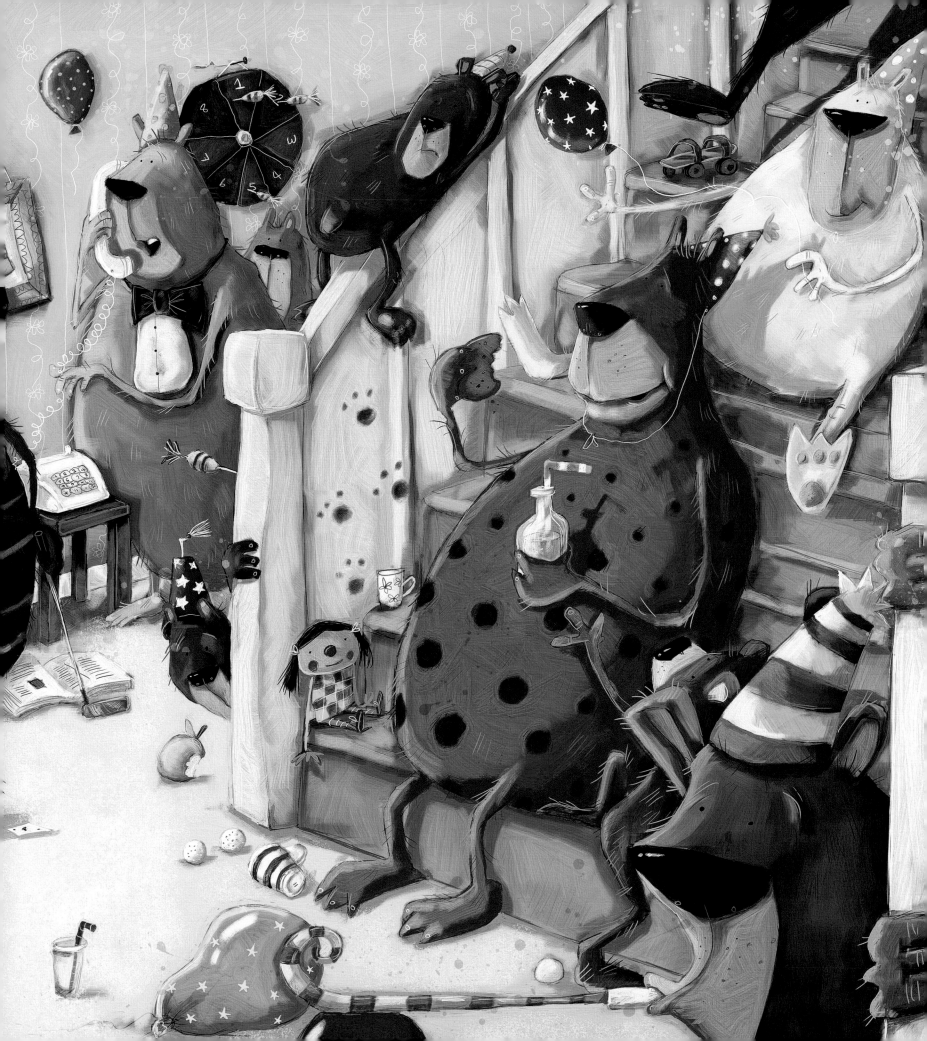

Five bears were snoring in Ruby's bed.
"I'll sleep in the bath!"
Ruby said, grabbing a
blanket off the bears.

But there was a bear in the bath playing with boats. Two bears were lining up to get in the shower. Three bears were looking for towels. And the littlest of all the bears was curled up in the sink.

"THERE ARE TOO MANY BEARS!" cried Ruby.

"I thought there might be,"
said Ruby's bear. And he yelled:
"**BEARS OUT!**"

Straight away the
bears hurtled out
of Ruby's house.

Bears **climbed** through the windows.

Bears **squeezed** up the chimney.

Bears **shot** through the doors.

Bears **popped** out from under the floors.

Everywhere there were bears,
running off into Bear Wood!

"Now you've only
one bear left,"
said Ruby's bear.

"One bear
is just what
I wanted,"
said Ruby.